PICTURES BY BARBARA MOSSMANN
STORY BY WERNER FARBER

Pig Trouble

HAMISH HAMILTON • LONDON

Wild Pig and his friends lived in a little wood on the edge of a lonely road. Every day they thought of new games to play. But whenever Wild Pig romped in the mud patch, his friends ran off. They didn't want to make pigs of themselves, splashing around in the mud.

One day Wild Pig heard a shrill squeaking
echo through the trees. A strange pink animal
was lying in the road!
Wild Pig ran to fetch his friends.

"It's a fairy!" whispered Squirrel.

"More like a human," suggested Stag.

"Nonsense," said Fox. "It's only a pig."

"What do you mean, 'only'?" snapped Wild Pig
crossly. "Anyway, it doesn't look anything like me."

"It does, you know," said Fox, as he turned to go.

Wild Pig was curious. He sneaked up behind the strange animal. Perhaps it did look a little like him, after all.

Its nose was about right,   but it had a ridiculous curly tail.

And it was fat and pink and didn't have *any* hair.

What was it doing in Wild Pig's wood?

He'd better keep his eye on it!

How cheeky! The lop-eared stranger was
munching Wild Pig's chestnuts!

Now it was chatting with his friends!

And now it was sleeping under
Wild Pig's favourite tree!

"I've had enough!" roared Wild Pig angrily.
"You can't get away with this in *my* wood!
Get out! Go on, scram!"

The pink pig ran away as
fast as it could.
Splash!
It jumped straight into
Wild Pig's mud patch.
Splash!
Wild Pig jumped in
right behind it.

The two pigs wrestled

in the mud.

Squelch, squelch!

Then they threw mud-balls — splat!

Actually, they were having a lot of fun.

Wild Pig, Pink Pig and their friends
live in a little wood on the
edge of a lonely road...

HAMISH HAMILTON LTD

Published by the Penguin Group
27 Wrights Lane, London W8 5TZ, England
Penguin Books USA Inc, 375 Hudson Street, New York, New York 10014, USA
Penguin Books Australia Ltd, Ringwood, Victoria, Australia
Penguin Books Canada Ltd, 10 Alcorn Avenue, Toronto, Ontario, Canada, M4V 3B2
Penguin Books (NZ) Ltd, 182-190 Wairau Road, Auckland 10, New Zealand

Penguin Books Ltd, Registered Offices: Harmondsworth, Middlesex, England

First published in Great Britain 1995 by Hamish Hamilton Ltd

Copyright © 1994 by K. Thienemanns Verlag, Stuttgart - Wien

1 3 5 7 9 10 8 6 4 2

British Library Cataloguing in Publication Data
CIP data for this book is available from the British Library

ISBN 0-241-13560-5

PRINTED IN BELGUIM BY

INTERNATIONAL BOOK PRODUCTION